JULES HOWARD LUCY LETHERLAND

THE WHO, WHAT, WHY OF ZOOLOGY

THE INCREDIBLE SCIENCE OF THE ANIMAL KINGDOM

WIDE EYED EDITIONS

CONTENTS

Inspiring | Educating | Creating | Entertaining

Brimming with creative inspiration, how-to projects and useful information to enrich your everyday life, Quarto is a favourite destination for those pursuing their interests and passions.

First published in 2023 by Wide Eyed Editions, an imprint of The Quarto Group.
1 Triptych Place, London, SE1 9SH, United Kingdom.
T (0)20 7700 6700 **www.Quarto.com**

A catalogue record for this book is available from the British Library.

ISBN 978-0-7112-7704-5
eISBN 978-0-7112-7707-6

The illustrations were created digitally
Set in Marons and Quicksand

Published by Debbie Foy
Designed by Myrto Dimitrakoulia • Edited by Alex Hithersay
Commissioned by Georgia Amson-Bradshaw
Production by Dawn Cameron

Manufactured in Guangdong, China TT122022

9 8 7 6 5 4 3 2 1

WHAT IS ZOOLOGY?

Why do animals behave the way they do? What are they saying to one another with their colours, songs and smells? And how do they shape the world we live in? Zoology is the science dedicated to answering questions like these.

Right now, as you read this book, zoology is happening all over the world. Every week, animal species are discovered – insects, whales, even dinosaurs – and weird and wonderful animal adaptations are newly described by scientists. There's always more to find out, so the world needs more ideas, more understanding and more zoologists.

Are you up to the job? If so, read on...

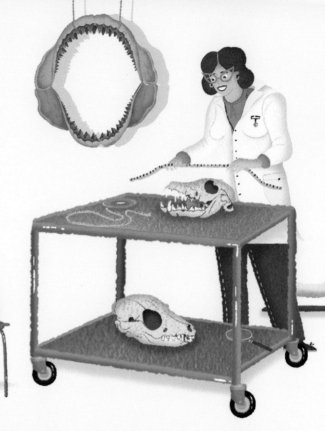

WHAT DO ZOOLOGISTS DO?

Zoologists try to learn new things about animals. What do they eat? Where do they lay their eggs? How do they interact with their habitats? Zoologists write down their observations and think of ways to test their ideas. Like all science, the best zoological discoveries are supported by lots of evidence.

USING THIS BOOK

Each chapter in this book looks at a different environment where zoology happens. First, you'll discover the animals **WHO** make their homes there, and amazing facts about how they live. Then, turn the page to learn **WHAT** zoologists do there to uncover the animal kingdom's secrets. Turn the page again to explore **WHY** zoologists do what they do, and the mysteries yet to be solved by science.

ORDER! ORDER!

Every living organism can be placed in groups, according to how closely related it is to other organisms. The most closely related groups are individuals within the same 'species' – all the individuals able to breed with one another. The next group is the 'genus', which is made up of closely related species.

Genus and species names are linked together to make an animal's scientific name. The grey wolf (whose species name is *lupus*) is related to other dog-like mammals, like coyotes and jackals (all in the genus *Canis*) and so the grey wolf's scientific name is *Canis lupus*.

A RACE AGAINST TIME...

Wild places are being destroyed faster than ever, because of the actions of humans. This threatens the lives of animals, large and small. Thankfully, zoologists can help! Many zoologists are involved in projects that keep track of wild animals and how endangered they are. Whales, gorillas and pandas are just some of the species that have been saved by zoologists, working closely with local communities and governments.

ZOOLOGY, THEN AND NOW

For hundreds of years, zoologists have studied animals to try to learn more about them. During this time, the techniques that they use have changed enormously. With technological advances and more people than ever having access to zoology, scientific discoveries are occurring at an incredible rate. Where will zoology go next?

Many zoologists used to work in dusty museums that kept their doors locked to the public. Only those considered worthy, through their reputation or level of education, were permitted entry. Most zoologists were men, because women were usually denied the education needed to become a zoologist.

Bones, fossils and stuffed specimens were very important to old-fashioned zoologists. Like library books, these could be studied in detail to learn new facts. However, they were sometimes lost or poorly looked after.

EVOLUTION REVOLUTION

By far the biggest shake-up in our understanding of animals came in 1859 with the publishing of a book, *On the Origin of Species*, by Charles Darwin. Darwin was the first to explain how species change very slowly over time, naturally, in a process called evolution. The book helped zoologists see that animals – including humans – can be close relatives of one another and that animal histories can be arranged in a kind of family tree.

To get samples of animals from around the world, zoologists used to ask travellers to look out for strange and unknown creatures and bring them home for a fee. But this often went against the wishes of local communities, who respected or even worshipped animals and did not want to see them taken.

To share their discoveries, zoologists of the past had to write letters to one another, which took lots of time. Sometimes conversations between zoologists could go on for years!

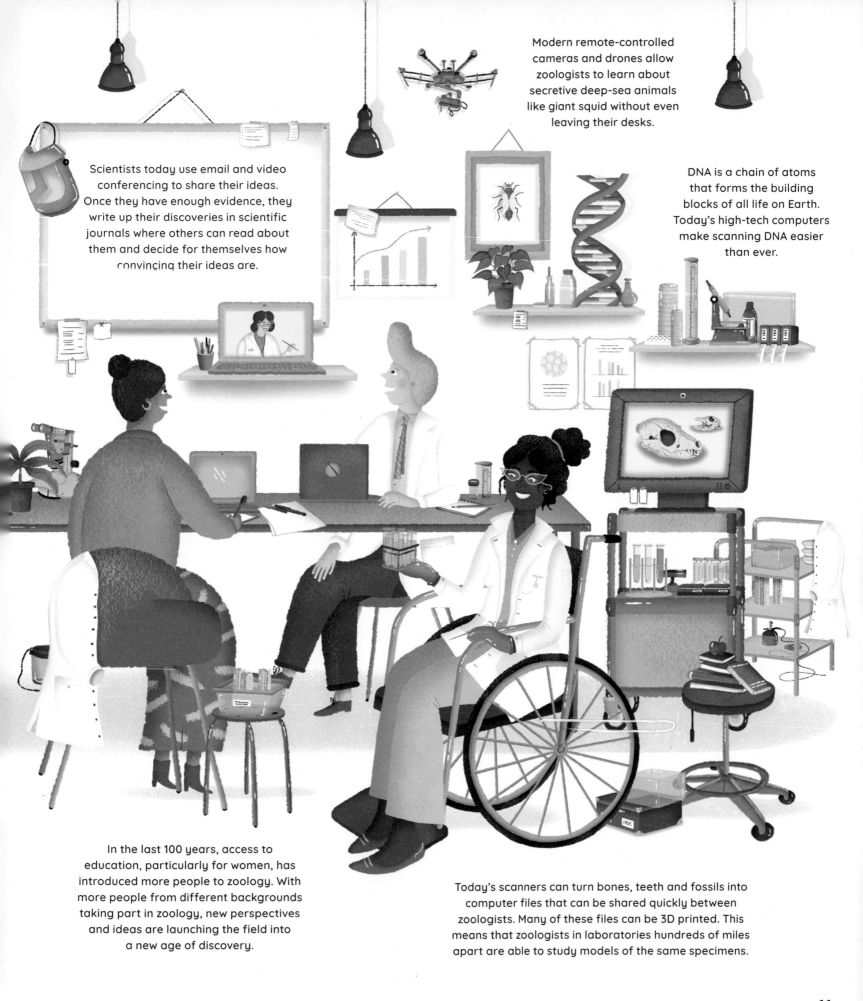

Modern remote-controlled cameras and drones allow zoologists to learn about secretive deep-sea animals like giant squid without even leaving their desks.

Scientists today use email and video conferencing to share their ideas. Once they have enough evidence, they write up their discoveries in scientific journals where others can read about them and decide for themselves how convincing their ideas are.

DNA is a chain of atoms that forms the building blocks of all life on Earth. Today's high-tech computers make scanning DNA easier than ever.

In the last 100 years, access to education, particularly for women, has introduced more people to zoology. With more people from different backgrounds taking part in zoology, new perspectives and ideas are launching the field into a new age of discovery.

Today's scanners can turn bones, teeth and fossils into computer files that can be shared quickly between zoologists. Many of these files can be 3D printed. This means that zoologists in laboratories hundreds of miles apart are able to study models of the same specimens.

11

TEMPERATE FORESTS

A quarter of Earth's ecosystems are found in temperate forests. These environments grow in regions where winter temperatures can dip below freezing. In the spring and summer, many animals travel from warmer countries to breed in temperate forests. Find out **WHO** lives here, amongst rustling leaves, beneath bark and in and out of tree roots!

TRICK OR TREAT

Squirrels store nuts and seeds during summer and autumn, preparing for winter when food is scarce. If rivals are watching, a squirrel will pretend to bury its nuts in one place, then hide them elsewhere when no one is looking! This keeps its winter supplies safe.

EYE OF NEWT

Newts can regrow lost body parts! In a matter of months, they can regenerate bits of their tail, jaws, eyes – even their heart. This adaptation helps newts survive in a habitat where predators are all around.

CALL THE CAVALRY

When caterpillars munch on the leaves of some trees, the leaves produce an odour that attracts tiny wasps. These wasps inject eggs into the caterpillars, from which hatch hungry grubs that eat them alive. Both the wasp and tree benefit from this unique arrangement.

CODE-BREAKERS

When hunting, bats fire sounds into the air and listen to how they rebound off nearby objects, including moths – their favourite prey. This is called echolocation. The tiger moth has a unique trick to get around this. It produces clicks from its abdomen that jam the bat's hunting frequency.

SAFETY IN NUMBERS

For most of their lives, periodical cicadas live as babies, or nymphs, in the soil. After up to 17 years, they all emerge to breed. Each acre of forest is flooded with more than a million adult cicadas. The sheer number of cicadas overwhelms and confuses predators, giving the next generation a better chance of surviving.

VENOM VENGEANCE

Opossums are well-protected from the venomous snakes that live in temperate forests. If bitten, chemicals in the opossum's blood attach to molecules of snake venom and break them down. Armed with this superpower, opossums regularly hunt snakes.

MEGA-MIGRATIONS

In the spring and summer, when energy from the sun is at its peak, food chains in temperate forests burst into life. Millions of spectacular insects such as monarch butterflies migrate thousands of kilometres to take advantage of the spoils. Birds like hummingbirds and swallows also travel across continents to join the feast.

13

Ecosystem Explorers

In winter, temperate forests can get very cold. Some animals hibernate, sleeping for most of the winter months. Those that do not hibernate need to find enough food to keep healthy and warm. Look up high and down low to discover **WHAT** these zoologists are doing to discover the secrets of their survival.

FEATHERY FUN

Using pulleys and ropes, this zoologist has set up a treetop hide where she can record bird songs with a microphone. She wants to know why different bird species sing at different times of the day.

WADER WATCHERS

Long rubber boots called waders allow these zoologists to remain dry as they stride into ponds and rivers to collect water samples. In a laboratory, they will scan the water for signs of rare salamander DNA.

WAYWARD WEEVIL

At one end of this fallen tree, hundreds of beetle grubs are exposed. These scientists are searching for a weevil species that has accidentally come here from a distant continent, bringing with it a mysterious tree disease. In recent years, 'invasive species' like these have been behind 40 per cent of animal extinctions.

LOOKING FOR LYNX

The lynx is one of this forest's most secretive predators. To walk through snow and wet mud, it has large padded paws. Could these be footprints? If so, these scientists can use them to estimate the number of lynx that live here.

TREETOP TWITTERING

This jackdaw family is playing while a zoologist watches. She is trying to understand how play might help jackdaws survive. Is it to learn about their environment? To work out who's boss? Or is play simply about fun?

INVASIVE SPECIES

As they move from place to place, humans can accidentally bring a range of animal hitchhikers with them. These include rats, who eat native wildlife or spread new diseases in their habitats. Insects such as wood-boring grubs and predatory beetles or wasps can also cause big problems. Each year, the cost to farming communities caused by invasive insects is more than 60 billion pounds.

SUCCESS STORY

These ibex lock horns in battle while scientists watch through binoculars. At one point, just 100 of these impressive mammals remained on Earth. They have been reintroduced, and now, thanks to the hard work of scientists, there are more than 50,000.

MUTANT MYSTERY

In most parts of the world, common lizards give birth to live babies, but here they lay eggs. Are these local lizards mutants, or are they evolving to become a new species? By sampling their DNA, scientists hope to find out more.

15

FORESTS FOREVER!

Temperate forests are spread throughout the world, so there are lots of places for zoologists to explore and protect. **WHY** are they so important to science? Let's find out!

Temperate forests become very dry in the summer months, so forest fires are a big threat. Some forests recover from fires quickly – new shoots grow fast and many animals return. But other forests can take decades to recover. Many zoologists are keen to see patches of forest better connected with one another. This means that, should one region burn, animals can escape to other parts of the forest to shelter. Tree-lined bridges have been used in some countries to link forests separated by roads.

Beavers used to be very common in temperate woodlands found across Europe, but hunting for their fur and meat almost drove them to extinction. Zoologists have been reintroducing them in the UK. Beavers build dams on streams and rivers, which creates ponds and small lakes and reduces the likelihood of floods farther downstream. These ponds become habitats for insects and amphibians. Some zoologists would like to reintroduce other lost animals, including wolves and lynx. To do this, they need to know more about how predators like these may shape their ecosystems in future.

STILL TO SOLVE

Who's a clever corvid? In recent years, crows, ravens, jackdaws, magpies and jays (a group known as corvids) have amazed zoologists with their ability to learn and communicate. Some species can wield sharpened sticks to get at hidden fruits and nuts, and recognise specific human faces, such as angry farmers, and warn others about them. Some flocks even seem to mourn their dead, gathering around a dead bird and making lots of noise. Are these funerals, as some zoologists argue? Are the crows curious, or even hungry? Or is something else going on?

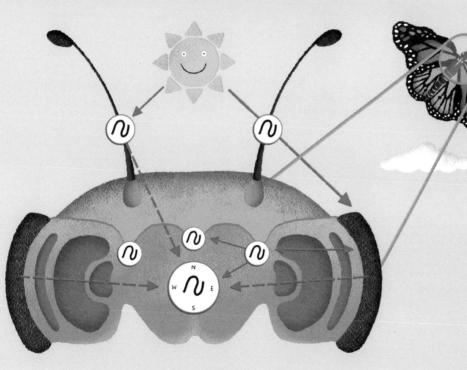

NEW TO SCIENCE

How does the monarch butterfly, with a brain no bigger than a grain of rice, navigate roughly 4,800 kilometres across North America? Inside the butterfly's antennae is a kind of 'clock' that tells its brain when and where to go. As it flies, the butterfly's eyes measure the sun's position on the horizon so that they can maintain the correct direction at all times. This 'clock' is wired into its DNA, meaning that even monarchs raised in captivity by scientists have proven capable of finding their way back to wintering grounds in Central America.

Few spiders are cuter than *Maratus jactatus*, discovered in 2015 by scientists in Queensland, Australia. The male of this pea-sized species (known locally as the sparklemuffin) boasts vibrant colours on its abdomen, which it waves around to impress passing females, like a peacock.

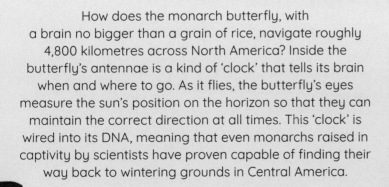

TROPICAL RAINFORESTS

Tropical rainforests are natural cities, bustling with life from the dank forest floor to the sky-scraping treetops. They grow along the equator, where there is lots of sun and rain all year round. They cover 6 per cent of Earth's surface, but are home to around 80 per cent of all animal and plant species. **WHO** lives in these green metropolises?

SNAKE SPURS

The ancestors of snakes had legs. As they evolved, the legs were lost, enabling them to slither through tight spaces easily. But in species like the green anaconda, the legs remain as tiny stubs near the bottom of the body, called spurs. Males use their spurs to tickle females into noticing them.

PERILOUS POOING

Once a week, tree-dwelling three-toed sloths make a death-defying descent to the forest floor... to go to the toilet. By this point, their poo and wee weigh about a third of their total body weight! Their droppings are signposts to other sloths, letting them know their whereabouts and whether they are ready to mate.

ZAP!

To keep predators away, the electric eel can produce a 650-volt blast of electricity – that's five times more powerful than a standard electric socket. Cells in its body can quickly change their chemical contents to generate an electric current.

RAUCOUS RAINFORESTS

Howler monkeys are some of the loudest land animals in the world. Their hoots are comparable to a jet plane taking off! The monkey makes these noises using an echo chamber, called the hyoid, attached to its voice box. These calls ring out for 4 kilometres and help howler monkeys keep others away from their territory.

BLOOD RADAR

Blood-sucking vampire bats can 'see' heat. Special patches of cells near the nose are very sensitive to changes in temperature and these guide vampire bats to the juiciest parts of the animal they are feeding on, where the blood is closest to the surface. Pain-killing chemicals in the bat's saliva make the bite painless.

TERRIBLE TALONS

The harpy eagle has the longest talons of any bird. Twice as long as a human finger, the eagles use their talons to seize and carry sloths and monkeys to their treetop nests to eat. They outsize the claws of many predatory mammals, including tigers.

POISON PREY

The golden poison frog is covered in enough toxic mucus to kill 10 people. It recycles the venom of the stinging and biting insects it eats, and then sheds these chemicals through its skin. Its eye-catching colours warn other animals of its deadliness, a form of defence known as aposematism.

19

RAINFOREST RANGERS

Rainforests are tough going! To work here, zoologists need to stay focused. Not only must they contend with thick trunks and thorny vines, they need to fend off biting insects and thirsty leeches. Teamwork is essential to keep from getting lost. But apart from navigating the difficult terrain, *WHAT* important work do zoologists do here?

DRONE DEFENCE

A drone glides high above the trees, controlled by a zoologist nearby. It is taking photos that will be used to make a map of the area, safeguarding its future.

CAIMAN CATCHERS

These zoologists are slowly moving their torch beams across the surface of the water. When the light shines on a black caiman, cells at the back of the caiman's eyes reflect the light back. This makes these nocturnal hunters easier to count.

MOON MIMICRY

Many night-flying insects mistake artificial light sources for the moon, which they use to navigate. These scientists have put a powerful lightbulb in front of a white sheet and are recording the species that appear. Some of these insects have never been seen before by human eyes.

CLAWS AND CLUES

These enormous scratch marks are the work of a giant armadillo. With banana-sized claws, armadillos smash open termite mounds and ant nests to eat the eggs and larvae inside. This scientist is measuring the scratch marks to learn the size of armadillos that live nearby.

FROG FINDERS

These scientists are looking for an elusive frog which is calling from the water's edge. By approaching the sound from different angles and pointing at where the noise is coming from, they can pinpoint the frog's exact location – this is called triangulation.

CAMERA SHY

This camera trap has been set up to take photos of secretive jaguars. Scientists will use the images to work out how many jaguars might remain in the forest.

SEED SPREADERS

This scientist is looking through howler monkey droppings for seeds from fruit that the monkey has recently eaten. Three-quarters of rainforest trees provide fruits and seeds for mammals to eat. Mammals spread the seeds far and wide in their droppings, enabling more trees to grow.

SLOUGH SLEUTHING

This scientist is examining a snake's shed skin, or slough (pronounced 'sluff'), to work out what species it came from. Later, the slough will be sent to a museum where other experts will investigate.

LAYERS UPON LAYERS

Scientists separate the rainforest into four main zones. Bathed in sunlight, the emergent layer is where leaves get the most energy and where birds nest. Below this, the canopy layer, thick with branches and vines, provides a roof-like space protecting the understorey, where large leaves collect the fragments of any light that still penetrates. Below, the forest floor is alive with insects, especially ants and beetles, who recycle the waste that falls from above.

MYSTERIOUS MILLIONS

Most rainforest animals have only been seen once or twice by humans, and millions of species remain unknown. In fact, as many as 80 per cent of rainforest animals (mostly insects, spiders and frogs) might not yet have a scientific name. To discover more about these animals, zoologists venture into remote parts of rainforests. Here are some of the reasons **WHY** zoologists are so devoted to these mysterious places.

A quarter of medicines come from chemicals first discovered in rainforest plants and animals. These include treatments for malaria that come from the bark of the cinchona tree and painkillers made from the toxins of poison dart frogs. Animals often provide the blueprints for new medicines and then chemists work to recreate their chemicals in the laboratory.

One of the biggest questions in zoology is: exactly how many species are out there? At the moment, scientists have named 1.6 million species of plants and animals but there are millions yet to be discovered. Scientists sometimes try to find as many new species as possible in a single square kilometre and use this number to predict how many exist across an entire region. This technique, alongside others, suggests that Earth is possibly home to a staggering 8.7 million species.

SHRINKING RAINFORESTS

Scientists are under pressure to work fast. Rainforests are being lost to deforestation all over the world, as trees are cut down for timber or to clear space for farming. In the Amazon alone, 10,000 square kilometres of rainforest is lost each year – that's an area half the size of Wales. The more that scientists understand about the species that live there, the better they are able to advise governments on the importance of rainforests, encouraging them to invest in strategies that protect the environment and benefit local people.

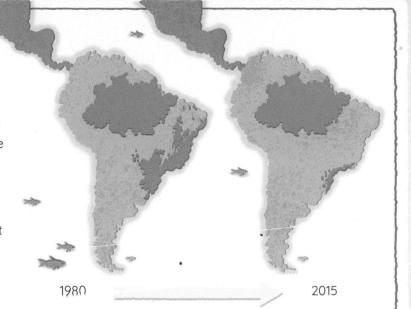

1980   2015

Most newly discovered animals are insects, which are the largest animal group on the planet. But occasionally, bigger animals are discovered for the first time. In 2013, zoologists were amazed to discover a new species of carnivorous mammal named the olinguito (pronounced oh-lin-ghee-toe) living in South America. This secretive weasel-like animal lives in the rainforest canopy, where it feeds on insects, fruits and nectar.

NEW TO SCIENCE

Who names species? The general rule in zoology is, if you discover something no one has seen before, you get to give the animal its scientific name. This strange rainforest frog, discovered in 2021, has the scientific name *Synapturanus zombie*. The name was chosen because its discoverers had to dig through the soil with their hands like zombies to find it!

ESERTS

Deserts are dry regions where rain rarely falls. Even with burning temperatures and searing winds, deserts are home to thousands of animals *WHO* find a way of life here. Some race over hot sand. Some dig through it. Every single species is a master of survival, living life at the extremes.

MONITOR MUNCH

STAY BACK! For years, the bite of the desert monitor lizard has been feared for the flesh-eating bacteria that live in its mouth. But these lizards also have venom-making glands in their jaws, which means they can deliver a painful bite like some snakes. These evolved from the glands that their ancestors used to make saliva.

STRIDING TO SUCCESS

Stand-off! Though cheetahs can sprint in short bursts at 130 kilometres per hour (as fast as a car on a motorway!), ostriches are better long-distance runners. Over many kilometres, ostriches can reach 55 kilometres per hour. To fuel their muscles with extra oxygen, ostriches have blood cells three times larger than those of humans.

JUMPING JERBOAS

Desert animals must travel long distances to find food. To save energy, the jerboa, a small rodent, uses a two-legged hop that limits its contact with the hot sand. Kangaroos and wallabies have a similar adaptation. When different species separately evolve similar features to do the same job, it is called convergent evolution.

FOSSIL FIELDS

Erosion is the process by which rocks are worn away by wind, rain or seawater. Rocks buried in deserts erode slowly because there is less rainfall. This makes deserts excellent places to find fossils – including of early humans and dinosaurs. In 2020, a complete fossil tail of *Spinosaurus* was found in the Sahara, in Northern Africa. It suggested that *Spinosaurus* was a swimming predator!

ACHOO!

In their packs, African wild dogs spend much of the day sheltering from the hot sun. When they awaken, leaders in the group rouse the troops by letting out sneezing noises. Three confident sneezes is usually all it takes for the whole group to stand up, shake off sleep and set off to hunt.

RAPID ARACHNIDS

Camel spiders can run ten times faster than the spiders you might find at home. Though they look like spiders, they are part of a wider group called arachnids. In deserts, camel spiders often scurry up to humans. Thankfully, they are simply looking for shade – not out to eat us!

STINKY STARGAZERS

Many species of dung beetle roll dung into balls which they wheel home to feed to their grubs. To find their way back to their burrows, dung beetles keep an eye on the sky. They use the Sun, Moon and even the Milky Way as reference points.

25

SEEKERS IN THE SAND

Contending with burning midday sun and freezing nights, zoologists have to be well prepared to explore the world's deserts. **WHAT** zoologists do here requires a good hat, plenty of water and a sense of adventure!

RINGLEADERS

Oases are patches of deserts where there is enough water for plants to grow, providing precious habitats out of the scorching heat. When travelling thousands of kilometres from Southern Africa to Europe, many birds use oases as a pitstop. The zoologists in this hide are looking for numbered rings that other scientists attached to the birds' legs weeks before. The rings tell what country the bird first flew from, helping us to learn more about secret migration routes.

TORTOISE TUNNELS

The African spurred tortoise digs tunnels that can be almost as long as a bowling alley! When the tortoise moves out, small mammals and reptiles move into these burrows. These scientists have attached a camera to a remote-controlled car to investigate the new residents.

STILT STRIDERS

This zoologist is trying to prove that some ants navigate back to their burrows by counting their steps. He has attached tiny stilts onto some of the ants to make their legs longer. If the ants are really counting their steps to get home, he predicts that the ants with stilts will end up walking past the nests because their strides are longer.

ANCIENT ANCESTORS

While looking for rare beetles, this zoologist has uncovered fossil footprints from humans who lived long ago. She is carefully covering them up with sheets to protect them from the dry wind, until scientists arrive from a nearby museum to investigate them.

FUNGUS FIGHTERS

This Sahara frog is being carefully wiped with a cotton bud. Later, a laboratory will examine the DNA on the cotton bud to see whether the frog has a fungal disease called chytridiomycosis (pronounced kit-rid-ee-oh-my-co-sis). This disease has caused many amphibian extinctions in recent years.

DESERT SWAMPS

Using a sieve, this scientist is collecting fish fossils. Her findings may confirm theories that, until the last few thousand years, this part of the Sahara was a wetland, brimming with life.

SHIFTING SANDS...

Earth's ecosystems can change very quickly. It took less than two thousand years for the wetlands of Northern Africa to become the dry deserts we know today. Scientists are still trying to understand more about what is behind dramatic changes like these (known as desertification). Is it down to changing wind patterns? Or changes in Earth's atmosphere? And will desertification become more common as Earth's climate continues to change? In time, scientists will have answers.

27

DEMYSTIFYING THE DESERTS

For centuries, many deserts were simply too hot and dry to explore. Now, armed with exciting technologies, a new generation of zoologists braves the sands to discover more about desert animals. Find out **WHY**!

Many ape-like ancestors of humans lived in East Africa, where lots of fossils of their kind have been found. The most famous fossil is 'Lucy', the remains of a 3-million-year-old *Australopithecus* (pronounced ost-ra-low-pith-eh-cus). Yet questions remain about how some of those early humans moved out of Africa and exactly when they spread across the world. Through fossils, particularly in deserts, scientists will find answers!

This glider has solar panels on the top of its wings which charge a battery in the cockpit. When the glider comes down to land, it can take off again using energy stored in the battery to power its thrusters. In future, solar-powered vehicles like these will help scientists explore the tough interiors of deserts, where few explorers have travelled before.

By pulling its legs into a basket shape, the flic-flac spider of Morocco can roll across the desert sand like tumbleweed. By springing the joints in its legs as it moves, it can even power itself uphill. So efficient is this method of travel, that one day it may be copied and used in robots sent to explore far-off rocky planets.

On foggy mornings, this thirsty darkling beetle stands with its bottom pointing upwards at the sky. Microscopic bumps on its wing cases catch water molecules from the fog. These form droplets that flow down channels towards the beetle's mouth. By artificially creating these bumps in a laboratory and attaching them to special panels, scientists hope to harvest water in dry deserts. One day, this water could be used to help local farmers grow crops.

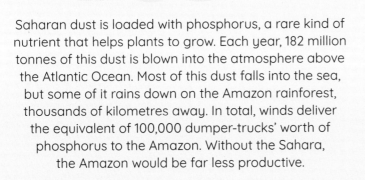

Saharan dust is loaded with phosphorus, a rare kind of nutrient that helps plants to grow. Each year, 182 million tonnes of this dust is blown into the atmosphere above the Atlantic Ocean. Most of this dust falls into the sea, but some of it rains down on the Amazon rainforest, thousands of kilometres away. In total, winds deliver the equivalent of 100,000 dumper-trucks' worth of phosphorus to the Amazon. Without the Sahara, the Amazon would be far less productive.

NEW TO SCIENCE

Discovered in the remote deserts of Iran in 2020, this new species of velvet spider (*Loureedia phoenixi*) was nicknamed the 'Joker Spider', after its vivid colours reminded its discoverer of the infamous comic-book villain. So far, only two males of this species have been found. The females, thought to live in underground burrows, remain unknown.

GRASSLANDS

Grasslands are found on all continents except Antarctica. In total, these rich ecosystems cover approximately one-third of all land on Earth. Most grasslands are semi-natural or agricultural (planted by farmers) but many remain wild places that bustle with the elusive creatures **WHO** call them home.

TOOTHY TOOLS

As elephants evolved over millions of years, two of their incisor teeth became very long indeed – they are tusks. Tusks are signs of health and strength, and help elephants pull down shrubs or dig up clumps of tender grass to eat.

F-ANT-ASTIC FEEDING

Sloth bears have long, muscular lips which they use like a straw to hoover up insects. They can completely close their nostrils to give them extra vacuuming power. In a single meal, a sloth bear can eat up to 10,000 ants.

WHAT A SHOW-OFF!

This male lesser florican is showing off to nearby females, performing an elaborate dance that involves jumping high above the grasses, arching its head back and gliding downwards gracefully. Though it stands 50 centimetres tall, it can leap more than 2 metres high. That's like an adult human jumping over a giraffe's head!

TEETH-READING

Like an ID badge, animal teeth can help zoologists identify their finds very quickly. Mammals have milk and adult teeth that come in three shapes: incisors, canines and molars. Sharks have rows of sharp teeth, and crocodile teeth, which resemble those of dinosaurs, can regrow again and again from out of the jawbone.

SOFTSHELL SWIMMERS

Not all turtles have hard shells. Some, like the Indian narrow-headed softshell turtle, have a shell that is smooth and leathery. Its lightweight armour lets this reptile move more freely through water. In the blink of an eye, it uses its long and flexible neck to fling its beaked jaws at unsuspecting prey.

DEADLY PRECISION

The Bengal tiger's pointy canine teeth are ten times the size of a house cat's. When a tiger has an animal in its jaws, special nerves in each canine allow it to feel for the gaps between the neck bones of its prey. By biting down in exactly the right place, the tiger can kill its meal in an instant.

GHARIAL GRUNTS

The gharial is a survivor from the age of dinosaurs. Male gharials have on their noses a strange bowl-like chamber called a ghara, which makes their calls travel further. Their strange hissing sounds can travel for more than 75 metres under the water – that's almost as long as a football pitch!

GRASSLAND GO-GETTERS

Prairies, steppes, savannahs, pampas – there are many different kinds of grassland but they have one thing in common: diversity! A total of 1 square metre of soil here can support over 70 species of plant, each home to a collection of insects and other invertebrates, which provide food for hungry predators. **WHAT** can zoologists do to learn about them all?

KICKING UP A FUSS

By kicking up mud from the bottom of the stream and netting the animals that flee, these zoologists gain a closer look at the invertebrates that live in this water. This is called kick-sampling. If lots of different species live here, it suggests that the water has not been polluted.

FEEDING FRENZY

Once or twice a year, a termite queen lays special eggs that hatch into royal sons and daughters. In their thousands, they will fly from her nest to start their own colonies. These scientists are writing down observations about the hungry birds that dip in and out of the swarm to eat the royal bugs.

OUTDOOR LESSONS

This zoologist is teaching some local school children about the Manipur bush quail, a secretive bird that likes to hide among the grasses. The bird was thought extinct until 2006, when it was rediscovered.

CHOPPER CHASE

Here, a zoologist has teamed up with a local helicopter pilot. They are flying off to investigate reports of Indian rhinos being tracked by poachers eager to cut off their horns and sell them illegally.

NET GAINS

By waving large nets over the top of the grasses, zoologists from a nearby museum are collecting flies and beetles which they will identify using microscopes and magnifying glasses. This is called sweep-netting. Once identified and recorded, the animals will be released.

LEOPARD LOOKOUT

To learn more about the secretive clouded leopard, zoologists have set up hundreds of camera traps in the area. Each camera trap will take thousands of photos of all sorts of animals. A team of volunteers at a local museum will look over the photos. Will these images provide evidence that clouded leopards live here?

GRASS, YOU ASK?

After dinosaurs went extinct, grasses evolved and swept across the world like a new fashion trend. The secret of their success is the way they grow. If a herbivore snips at grass leaves with its teeth, the leaves can continue to grow from the roots up. This makes grasses tough and, once established, hard to remove. Grassland soils are often very rich in nutrients. This is because the long roots of grasses hold soil in place, locking nutrients underground for other plants and animals to make use of.

SECRETS OF THE SAVANNAH

Being rocky and sometimes mountainous, grasslands can be tough to explore. Many grasslands can only be charted on foot and some can only be crossed on horseback. So **WHY** bother? Though the going is tough, zoologists that make the journey are often rewarded for their efforts with wondrous new discoveries.

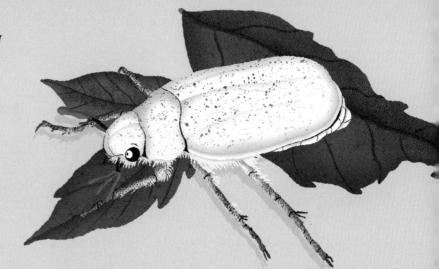

Whiter-than-white! This super-white beetle (*Cyphochilus*) is covered in tiny scales that scatter light in many directions at once. This makes a bright white colour that is unmatched in nature. Scientists have recreated these microscopic scales in laboratories. Their aim is to make a natural white paint that does not require lots of environmentally damaging chemicals to make.

By counting wild animals each year, zoologists can understand more about the speed at which threatened animals like Indian rhinos are disappearing. These figures feed into a computer database that monitors thousands of different species. The most threatened animals are labelled 'Vulnerable', 'Endangered' or 'Critically Endangered'. This helps governments know where to focus their much-needed efforts.

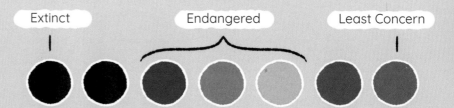

Extinct   Endangered   Least Concern

Zoologists have argued for more than a century about why zebras have stripes. Some say that stripes help zebras camouflage against grasses. Others think that stripes help zebras maintain their body heat. Some have even argued that stripes help individual zebras recognise one another. Now, zoologists think they have the answer. Scientists dressed up horses in zebra costumes, and noticed that blood-sucking flies found it harder to locate them. The stripy patterns trick the flies into thinking there is no surface to land on and so, confused, they look elsewhere.

Can you speak meerkat? In recent years, there has been a revolution in our understanding of secret animal languages. Many of these discoveries have come about by recording animal sounds and then playing them back through a loudspeaker and watching what happens. This is called a playback experiment. Playback experiments have shown that meerkats have their own simple language. An urgent yapping noise means 'WATCH OUT, EAGLE!' and tells meerkats to scan the sky for approaching threats. Likewise, a nervous chattering noise means 'SNAKE!' and tells them to form a gang that will chase away any approaching snakes.

NEW TO SCIENCE

A photo of this secretive snake was posted on social media by a student in the Himalayas who spotted it while searching for backyard reptiles. The image was seen by an Indian zoologist who suspected it of being a new species of egg-eating snake, known as a 'kukri' snake. After getting hold of another specimen, the zoologist was proven correct. The Churah Valley kukri snake, named in 2021, uses its curved back teeth to crush eggs, before greedily swallowing the contents.

TUNDRA

An icy world sparks into life! For most of the year, the tundra is a frozen landscape but for a few weeks in summer, animals are everywhere. Most tundra is found in northern polar regions, but tundra also exists on remote islands in the southern hemisphere, such as the Auckland Islands, between New Zealand and Antarctica. Discover **WHO** lives in these far-flung regions.

DO THE SEALION SHUFFLE

Unlike other sealions, the whakahao can travel long distances on land, using its muscular flippers and flexible tail. To keep out of the icy wind, some whakahao shuffle 2 kilometres or more looking for the shelter of long grasses.

NOT JUST A FLUKE

Southern right whales play games using their giant tails, or 'flukes'. As if doing a handstand, they stick them up in the air and try to balance there. Some scientists think the whales use their flukes to catch the wind and 'sail' through the water.

BACK FROM THE DEAD

For almost 100 years, the Auckland rail was thought extinct until it was rediscovered in 1966. Today, only 1,500 individuals of this secretive flightless bird remain.

FOUR-LEGGED FOES

Many remote islands are home to groups of pigs or goats, introduced long ago by sailors who were hungry for meat. In many cases, these mammals forced threatened seabirds and penguins to nest elsewhere.

THE TREELESS TUNDRA

Most of the water in the tundra is found in a frozen layer known as permafrost which sits below the surface of the soil.

The roots of trees struggle to penetrate this icy layer, so most tundra habitats are home to flowers, shrubs and grasses, which have shorter roots.

NO PLACE LIKE HOME

Albatrosses are very faithful to their nesting places. One world-record-holding albatross, named Wisdom, is still returning to the same island after 70 years. Albatrosses like remote islands because predatory mammals (particularly rats) have trouble getting to them.

GUANO GRAFFITI

To keep their smelly droppings from stinking out the nest, penguins can shoot their poo more than a metre away. This pasty substance, which splashes like paint against the rocks, is called guano (pronounced gu-ah-no).

WEIGHTY WĒTĀ

The wētā (pronounced wet-tah) is a giant, flightless cricket. Weighing more than a sparrow, it is one of the heaviest insects in the world. One wētā species from the Auckland Islands is found nowhere else on Earth.

ISLAND ENDEMISM

Sometimes, owing to continental shifts or even freak storms, animals find themselves on remote islands where they continue their evolution away from others of their species. In time, they can evolve to become a species entirely unique to that island. Animals like this are called endemic species.

LOCAL WISDOM

In the last 20 years, half of all reindeer have disappeared. To protect those that remain, these zoologists are being given important lessons from indigenous people whose communities have managed these lands for thousands of years. Together, they hope to secure the reindeer's future.

CARIBOU CLUES

Each year, reindeer (also known as caribou) shed their old antlers and grow new ones. Zoologists can investigate chemicals found in shed antlers to work out where on the continent they grew. This helps them map reindeer migration routes.

COOLER CLIMES

Thermal cameras measure the heat given off by these playful Arctic foxes. This zoologist wants to understand whether climate change will cause some furry animals to migrate further north, where it is cooler, to keep from overheating.

ICY INVESTIGATORS

Making your way through the tundra is hard going! Not only are many of these remote places far from cities and towns, they are also prone to unpredictable weather. It may look sunny now, but within minutes, an ice storm is likely to arrive. **WHAT** are these zoologists braving the weather to do?

FROZEN DESERTS

Being near to polar regions, tundra is, for most of the year, a cold place where temperatures rarely rise above freezing. Just 25 centimetres of rain and snow fall here each year. That means tundra regions are drier than many deserts!

RODENT RESEARCH

This zoologist is checking wooden boxes designed to trap small mammals and keep them safe overnight. Each tiny vole or mouse she discovers will be weighed, measured and then released back into the undergrowth.

RHINO RELIC

These scientists have discovered a woolly rhinoceros that has been here for 10,000 years! In the tundra, the soil is so cold that the bacteria that normally eat dead animals cannot grow. This means animal bodies like this one can be frozen in time for thousands of years.

Wonders of the Wilderness

Almost one-tenth of the world's surface is taken up by tundra and most of it is completely unexplored. That means there are plenty of secrets left for future zoologists to find, which could unlock the answers to some of science's biggest questions.

Back from the dead! Some scientists are collecting DNA from the frozen remains of long-dead mammoths. They hope that, one day, we might bring them back from extinction. But not all scientists support this idea. Some argue that we no longer have habitats that could support these woolly giants, which would need enormous territories to live happily. Others argue that we should be spending money on the animals that are in danger of extinction now, not on bringing back species that had their time long ago. There is also the matter of ethics: is it fair on a genetically engineered baby mammoth to be brought up alone, without others of its kind?

ETHICS: A POWER FOR GOOD

Ethics committees make great zoology happen! These important groups of people are found in many research facilities and universities. Their job is to look over the work that scientists undertake and make sure it does not harm animals (or people and their communities) in an unfair manner.

In very low temperatures, ice crystals begin to form inside animal cells, then expand and split open the cells. This damages tissues and can cause death. But some insects, such as the snow flea, have evolved a trick to get around this. Snow fleas have special molecules in their cells that grab onto ice crystals when they are small and stop them from expanding. This amazing 'antifreeze' molecule is very interesting to scientists. One day, snow flea technology might be used to keep human bodies on ice for hundreds of years, so that they can later be brought back to life!

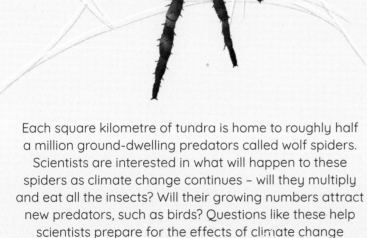

Each square kilometre of tundra is home to roughly half a million ground-dwelling predators called wolf spiders. Scientists are interested in what will happen to these spiders as climate change continues – will they multiply and eat all the insects? Will their growing numbers attract new predators, such as birds? Questions like these help scientists prepare for the effects of climate change in the years to come.

NEW TO SCIENCE

The rock beneath Antarctica's snow and ice contains a treasure trove of fossils, nearly all of them yet to be discovered. They include Ball's Antarctic tundra beetle, which lived on Antarctica when it was tundra 15 million years ago. In 2016, scientists discovered a fossilised wing casing of the beetle, shown here next to a living, related species.

TROPICAL REEFS

Welcome to the busiest place on Earth!
Coral reefs are underwater structures made from
the skeletons of corals. Though they resemble plants,
corals are actually animals. Just 1 per cent of the
world's oceans are home to coral reefs, yet one in
every four ocean species lives here. Discover **WHO** lurks
in this colourful, life-giving habitat.

BABY BOOM

Ocean sunfish can
lay 300 million eggs, each
not much bigger than a full stop in
this book. But in a matter of years,
this super-sized fish can reach more
than 3 metres wide and weigh as
much as a rhino. That's like
a human baby growing bigger
than a football stadium!

TENTACLE TEAMWORK

Octopuses have a large
brain in the body and bundles of
neurons – or mini 'brains' – in each
of their tentacles. When the female
reef octopus lays eggs, her brains
work together to hang each of the
50,000 eggs in an underwater
gallery, which she protects
with her life.

SUPER SHRIMP

This pistol shrimp packs
quite a punch! When it snaps
shut its claws, it generates a tiny
wave of bubbles that rockets
outwards like a sonic boom. It uses
this 'power-punch' to stun and
kill its prey. The sound is so
intense that it can interfere
with submarine
communications.

CORAL CASTLES

Coral reefs are made of thousands of tiny animals called polyps. These jellyfish-like animals, most no bigger than a coin, gather food with their tentacles. Polyps also house within them special algae that gathers light from the sun. In return for their safe housing, the algae give the coral polyp an extra boost of energy – an arrangement known as 'symbiosis'.

POO PARADISE

Using their large teeth, parrotfish bite off chunks of dead corals which they grind into dust and then swallow. They digest the nutritious parts and the rest comes out the other end in a cloud of fine, powdery white poo. Over thousands of years, this builds up. Many of the world's most beautiful beaches are made, almost totally, of parrotfish droppings!

EYES ON THE PRIZE

When sea snakes sleep, they hide their tails so that hungry predators don't see them poking out of the reef. The snakes have special light-sensing cells, like tiny eyes, on their tail. When these cells sense darkness, the snake knows its tail is safely tucked away.

43

CORAL CRUSADERS

To help keep the reef safe, these zoologists are searching for new species and keeping an eye on existing ones. Many scientists study how animals use corals to hide and grow, while others track the animals that visit the reef. *WHAT* high-tech tools and inventive ideas are needed to uncover the secrets of this unique underwater world?

REEF REVIEW

Every year zoologists take photos of this reef to track how much of it has become bleached, and measure the impact of climate change year-on-year.

HIDE-AND-PEEK

Many parts of the reef are too small for humans, so to see what lives in this crevice, zoologists have attached a camera to a long pole. Within lies a female reef octopus, guarding her 50,000 eggs.

GLOWING OFF

This lizardfish glows like a neon sign when a special kind of light, called ultraviolet or UV, shines on it. Many fish use these fluorescent bits to show off when the sun goes down. Zoologists use UV torches to recognise secretive reef fish more easily, meaning they can better monitor the health of the reef.

MANTA MARKS

When corals start to spawn, giant manta rays make their way across the ocean to feed on the millions of eggs the reef produces. Zoologists record the patterns on the rays' bellies so they can track them and protect their migration routes.

LUNAR LABS

These researchers are carefully removing corals to take to a laboratory, where they will be grown in a tank. By changing the light levels to mimic the Moon, they will encourage the corals to spawn and harvest the eggs to bring life to dead reefs.

WHALE WATCHERS

No one knows where whale sharks give birth to their pups. These zoologists are fitting a tracker on this young whale shark to see where she travels when she's ready to breed. The device talks to a satellite in space, which sends map coordinates to a zoology laboratory.

MIC DROP

Fish talk to each other in many ways, from chattering with their teeth to farting! This microphone records the calls of damselfish, one of the reef's noisiest residents, to try and work out what they mean.

WHAT IS CORAL BLEACHING?

When temperatures rise, coral polyps become stressed and flush out the algae that live inside them. This causes corals to lose their natural colours and become 'bleached'. Climate change is a major cause of coral bleaching. In recent years, over 90 per cent of Australia's Great Barrier Reef has been affected. Zoologists work hard to rescue the reefs that remain.

UNDER-SEA MYSTERIES

In recent years, lots of new discoveries have revealed more about the ocean and its incredible inhabitants. But there are still many mysteries out there. So **WHY** are zoologists so keen on coral reefs? Let's dive in!

Just like humans, dolphins sometimes get obsessed by the latest fashion trends. In Western Australia, in the 1980s, a dolphin pulled a sponge from the sea floor and wore it on its head. Later, other dolphins took to doing the same. Today, most dolphins in the area have taken up the fashion. 'Sponging' helps protect the dolphin's beak from sand and rocks while it digs for hidden fish. Today, mothers teach their babies the behaviour – an amazing example of non-human culture. Scientists are now trying to understand the other cultural traditions that whales and dolphins around the world might have.

Zoologists have recently discovered that, unlike other filter-feeding animals such as whales, the sieve-like gills of manta rays never get clogged. As water moves into the mouth of the ray, microscopic flaps on the gills make the water spin upwards like a tiny cyclone. This keeps particles from getting stuck. New discoveries like these may help engineers build vacuum-cleaners that can suck up tiny pieces of plastic from the sea.

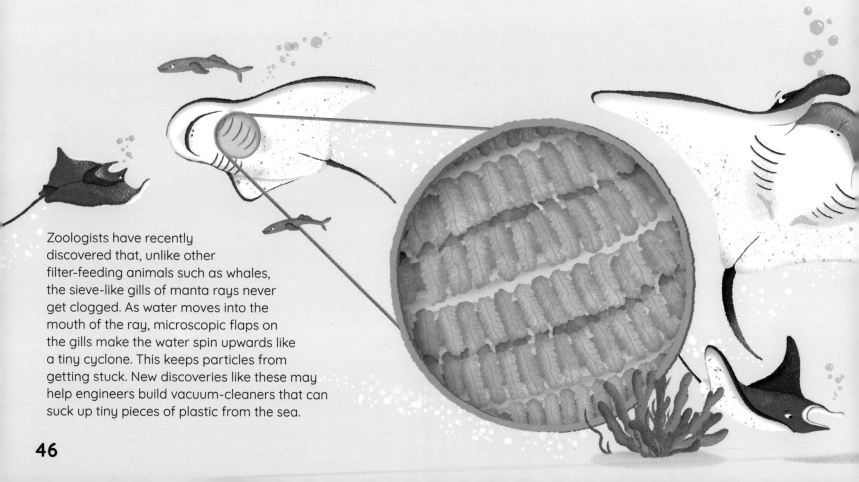

MARINE MYSTERIES

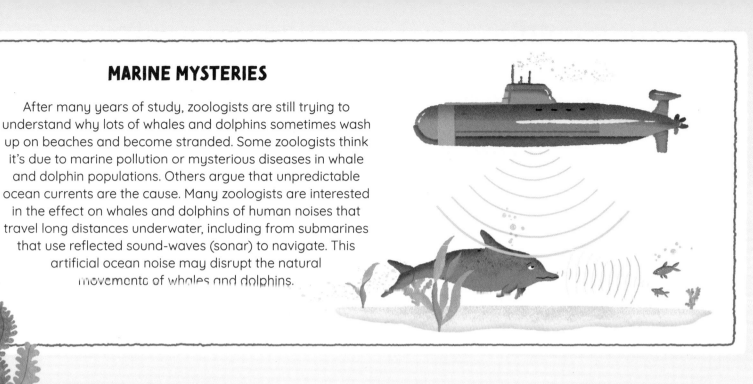

After many years of study, zoologists are still trying to understand why lots of whales and dolphins sometimes wash up on beaches and become stranded. Some zoologists think it's due to marine pollution or mysterious diseases in whale and dolphin populations. Others argue that unpredictable ocean currents are the cause. Many zoologists are interested in the effect on whales and dolphins of human noises that travel long distances underwater, including from submarines that use reflected sound-waves (sonar) to navigate. This artificial ocean noise may disrupt the natural movements of whales and dolphins.

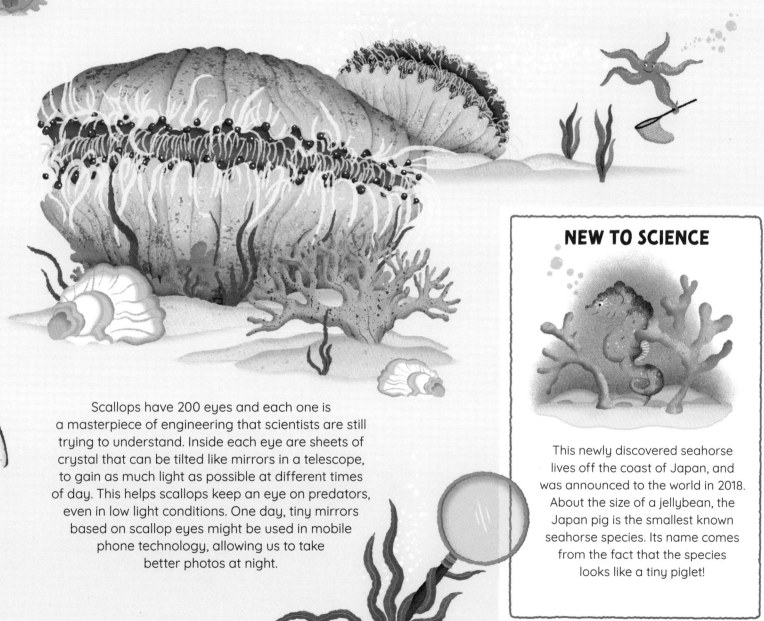

Scallops have 200 eyes and each one is a masterpiece of engineering that scientists are still trying to understand. Inside each eye are sheets of crystal that can be tilted like mirrors in a telescope, to gain as much light as possible at different times of day. This helps scallops keep an eye on predators, even in low light conditions. One day, tiny mirrors based on scallop eyes might be used in mobile phone technology, allowing us to take better photos at night.

NEW TO SCIENCE

This newly discovered seahorse lives off the coast of Japan, and was announced to the world in 2018. About the size of a jellybean, the Japan pig is the smallest known seahorse species. Its name comes from the fact that the species looks like a tiny piglet!

FOOD ON THE FLOOR

When whales and other large ocean animals die, the deep sea is where their bodies come to rest. Here, hundreds of different scavengers crowd together to take advantage of the spoils. First large animals arrive, including hagfish, octopus and grenadier fish, to feed on the blubber. Then come brittlestars and crabs which pick apart the internal organs. Lastly, the clean-up crew arrive – bone-eating snotflower worms. These strange scavengers become so numerous that they make the whale's bones look fuzzy from a distance.

LARVACEAN LAMPS

Half of all the glowing shapes in the deep ocean are tiny creatures known as larvaceans. When mixed together, chemicals in the body make these animals light up with a ghostly green glow. Blue and green light travels farthest through dark waters, so these colours are commonly used in the deep sea.

LIGHT SHOW!

It's a trap! A shrimp is coming over to investigate a strange glowing orb, which could be food. It doesn't yet know that this is a hungry firefly squid. Squid create light using cells called photophores. Inside these cells live colonies of light-producing bacteria.

DIZZY DINER

The corpse-eating hagfish has changed very little over millions of years. Its ancestors once fed on dead mosasaurs and ichthyosaurs in the age of dinosaurs. To tear off chunks of meat, hagfish bite and then spin around and around, like a sausage on a spit.

The deepest point on Earth
is at the bottom of the Mariana
Trench, near the island of Guam,
in the western Pacific Ocean. If
you placed Mount Everest upon this
seabed, and stacked twenty
Statue of Liberties on top, it
would still only just reach
the surface.

LOVE AT FIRST BITE

A tiny male anglerfish,
no bigger than a pea, has glued
itself to a passing female. He will live
out his days attached to her body
and eventually die after fertilising
her eggs. This strategy works in the
deep sea because it is rare for
fish of the same species to
chance upon one
another.

BRILLIANT
BRISTLEMOUTHS

Bristlemouths are the most
common bony animal on the planet.
Some scientists think there might
be more than a quadrillion of them
swimming in the depths. That means,
for every one of us, there are nearly
130,000 of them! Bristlemouths
catch tiny crustaceans
using their brush-like
teeth.

DEEP SEAS

A total of 95 per cent of the living space
on Earth is found 200 metres beneath the
ocean's surface, where light from the sun
cannot penetrate. Many years ago, scientists
considered these murky depths lifeless places,
but thanks to decades of discoveries, we now
know that the creatures **WHO** dwell down here
are just as varied as those above water.

49

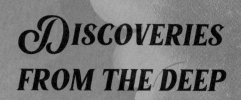DISCOVERIES FROM THE DEEP

Welcome to the hydrothermal vents – an ecosystem like no other! Like a chemistry experiment, these waters bubble with scorching temperatures amid a cocktail of rare minerals. Accessing these deep-sea communities is extremely difficult. Discover *WHAT* unique methods zoologists use here to find new and exciting species.

ALVIN THE EXPLORER

Some submarines have seen a lot of action! Known as Alvin, this hard-wearing vehicle has helped scientists explore untouched ecosystems for more than 40 years. It was the first to discover and explore hydrothermal vents up close, in 1977.

SNAIL STREAMING

This robot drone is controlled by scientists via a satellite link. It is producing a live video feed which can be viewed by thousands of scientists around the world. The camera has spotted a rare scaly-foot snail – the only known animal with a set of metallic scales, recycled from minerals found in the oceanic vents.

MASSIVE MUSSELS

Robotic arms collect a giant vent mussel, which will be placed in a special sample tube and taken back to the surface for laboratory scientists to examine.

TENTACLE TRICKS

Are these the tentacles of a titan? Giant squid can be longer than a school bus, yet sightings of these predators remain rare because they are highly suspicious of submarines and drones. These floating cameras shine red light, which squid can't see, at a fake jellyfish. This makes it give off light signals just like the real thing. A hungry giant squid has come over to investigate...

UNDER PRESSURE

In the deepest ocean, the pressure from the water is like being squished from all sides by 100 elephants! To stop this submarine from crumpling like a tin can, it has a thick titanium hull that is built like a tank.

FLOATING PHOTOSHOOT

This microscope is attached by a long wire to a boat hundreds of metres above. A flash bulb fires 60 times a second, collecting images of plankton: tiny organisms in the water that drift from place to place and are unable to move by themselves. Scientists want to know more about the plankton that live here and how they change throughout the year.

CATHEDRALS FROM CHAOS

Hydrothermal vents are like deep-water hot springs. They begin with super-heated groundwater, rich in rare minerals, bubbling out of volcanic rock into the icy waters of the deep. The sudden change from hot to cold causes the minerals in the groundwater to crystallise and become solid, forming cathedral-like spires and chimneys. Many of these structures are nibbled on by various strange bacteria, which then become food for animals including marine snails, clams and shrimp. Hey presto, a foodchain! Hydrothermal vents are the only places on Earth where an ecosystem has sprouted up without requiring any energy from the sun.

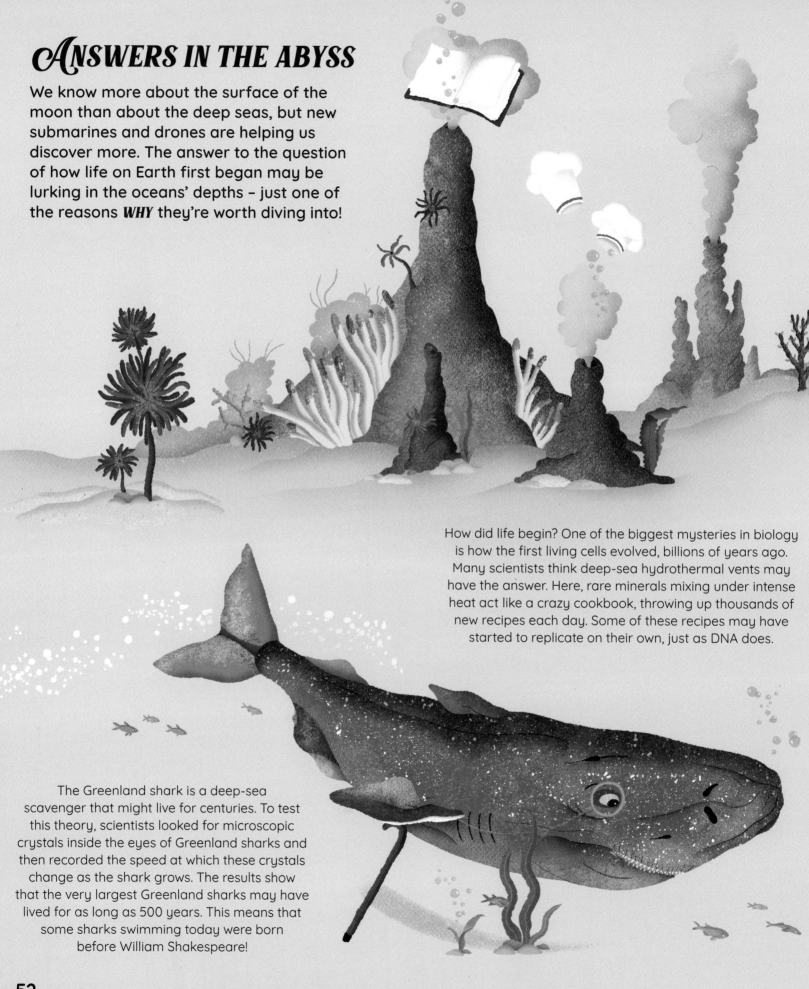

ANSWERS IN THE ABYSS

We know more about the surface of the moon than about the deep seas, but new submarines and drones are helping us discover more. The answer to the question of how life on Earth first began may be lurking in the oceans' depths – just one of the reasons **WHY** they're worth diving into!

How did life begin? One of the biggest mysteries in biology is how the first living cells evolved, billions of years ago. Many scientists think deep-sea hydrothermal vents may have the answer. Here, rare minerals mixing under intense heat act like a crazy cookbook, throwing up thousands of new recipes each day. Some of these recipes may have started to replicate on their own, just as DNA does.

The Greenland shark is a deep-sea scavenger that might live for centuries. To test this theory, scientists looked for microscopic crystals inside the eyes of Greenland sharks and then recorded the speed at which these crystals change as the shark grows. The results show that the very largest Greenland sharks may have lived for as long as 500 years. This means that some sharks swimming today were born before William Shakespeare!

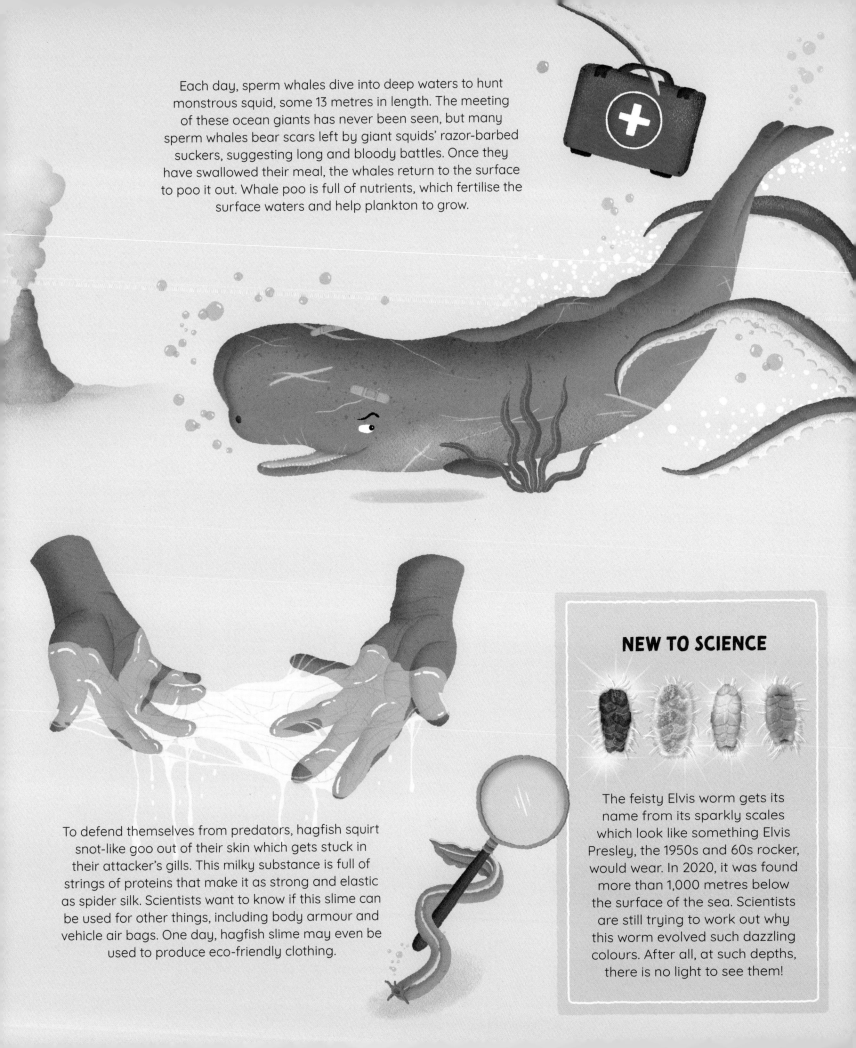

Each day, sperm whales dive into deep waters to hunt monstrous squid, some 13 metres in length. The meeting of these ocean giants has never been seen, but many sperm whales bear scars left by giant squids' razor-barbed suckers, suggesting long and bloody battles. Once they have swallowed their meal, the whales return to the surface to poo it out. Whale poo is full of nutrients, which fertilise the surface waters and help plankton to grow.

To defend themselves from predators, hagfish squirt snot-like goo out of their skin which gets stuck in their attacker's gills. This milky substance is full of strings of proteins that make it as strong and elastic as spider silk. Scientists want to know if this slime can be used for other things, including body armour and vehicle air bags. One day, hagfish slime may even be used to produce eco-friendly clothing.

NEW TO SCIENCE

The feisty Elvis worm gets its name from its sparkly scales which look like something Elvis Presley, the 1950s and 60s rocker, would wear. In 2020, it was found more than 1,000 metres below the surface of the sea. Scientists are still trying to work out why this worm evolved such dazzling colours. After all, at such depths, there is no light to see them!

IN THE LAB

Get ready for a tour of the tiniest! In laboratories, zoologists study animals big and small to see how they are influenced by the things around them, such as temperature and food. Laboratory scientists are especially interested in DNA, the chemical code found in all species on Earth. Good labs always make the welfare of the animals **WHO** live there, no matter how small, their top priority.

BUZZWORDS

'Flowers! Over there! A short distance from the nest!' That's what these displays, or 'waggle dances', say to other bees in the colony. Worker bees use this information to find sugary nectar which they bring back to feed the queen and her babies.

CARE IN THE COLONY

No leaf-cutter ant colony is complete without its own graveyard. Here, worker ants pile up their dead colony-mates in their thousands. Keeping dead ants far away from the nest protects the colony from horrible diseases.

DNA DREAM

See-through worms called nematodes are some of the most numerous animals on the planet. They outnumber humans 60 billion to one. Nematode DNA is easy to look at and tinker with, and they were the first animal whose DNA was completely mapped out by scientists.

PUDDLE PLANKTON

Using hundreds of tiny tentacles, a puddle-dwelling rotifer creates whirlpools that drag helpless bacteria into its hungry mouth. When food or water runs out, rotifers curl up into a ball and let the wind blow them to another puddle, where the feeding continues.

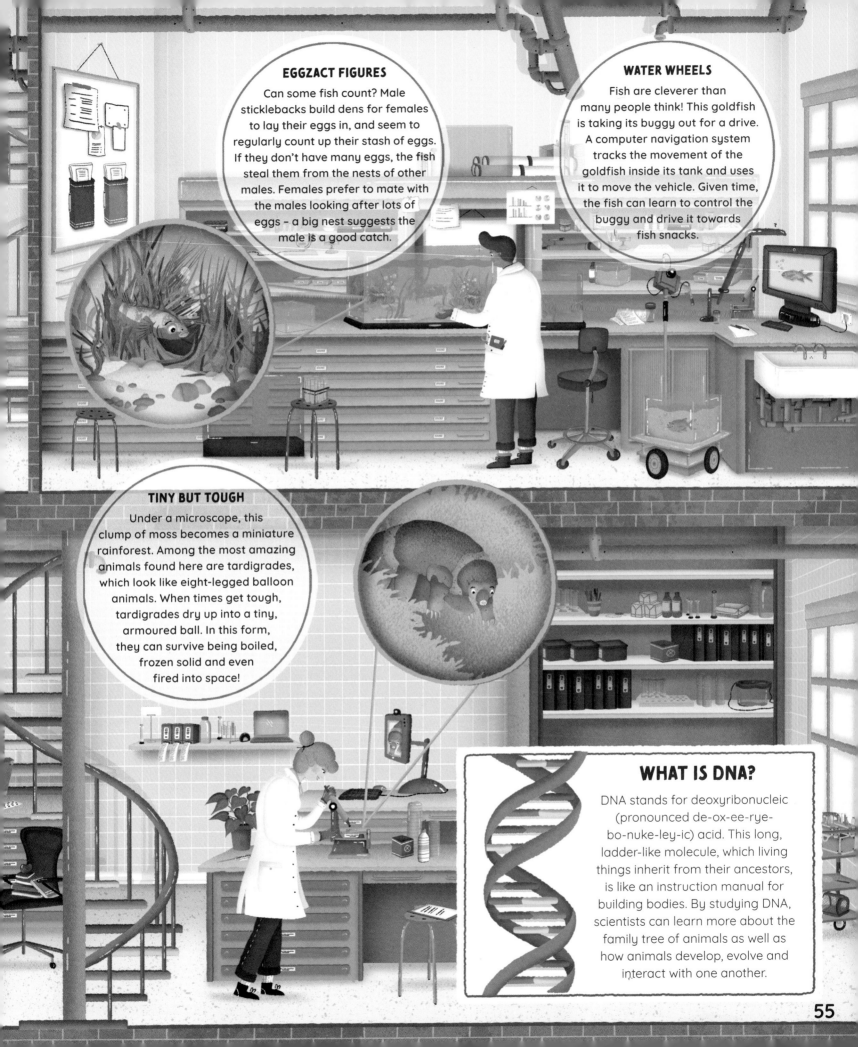

EGGZACT FIGURES

Can some fish count? Male sticklebacks build dens for females to lay their eggs in, and seem to regularly count up their stash of eggs. If they don't have many eggs, the fish steal them from the nests of other males. Females prefer to mate with the males looking after lots of eggs – a big nest suggests the male is a good catch.

WATER WHEELS

Fish are cleverer than many people think! This goldfish is taking its buggy out for a drive. A computer navigation system tracks the movement of the goldfish inside its tank and uses it to move the vehicle. Given time, the fish can learn to control the buggy and drive it towards fish snacks.

TINY BUT TOUGH

Under a microscope, this clump of moss becomes a miniature rainforest. Among the most amazing animals found here are tardigrades, which look like eight-legged balloon animals. When times get tough, tardigrades dry up into a tiny, armoured ball. In this form, they can survive being boiled, frozen solid and even fired into space!

WHAT IS DNA?

DNA stands for deoxyribonucleic (pronounced de-ox-ee-rye-bo-nuke-ley-ic) acid. This long, ladder-like molecule, which living things inherit from their ancestors, is like an instruction manual for building bodies. By studying DNA, scientists can learn more about the family tree of animals as well as how animals develop, evolve and interact with one another.

POWER PAINT

Many ocean-going birds have dark markings on the upper side of their wings. Do these markings somehow make bird wings more aerodynamic? To find out, this scientist is painting the upper side of these remote-control plane wings black, to see what effect this has on how long its batteries last.

WEB-BASED LEARNING

How does an animal as simple as a spider create such complicated webs? To explore this question, this camera records the simple steps that spiders go through when making their webs.

MYSTERIOUS MITES

On the slimy surface of slugs and snails, tiny spider-like animals called slug mites run around. But what do they feed on? And how many different species of slug mite are there? Above, a zoologist is collecting slug mite DNA to find out more...

ROBO RESEARCH

A robot fish is taking its first voyage! Zoologists are interested to know if its presence in the water will scare smaller fish into hiding. If so, robots like this could be used in streams to discourage the invasive mosquitofish, which regularly hunts tadpoles that need the stream for their survival.

LABORATORY LESSONS

In laboratories, zoologists use lots of high-tech equipment. Some of these gadgets uncover tiny animals that would otherwise be missed; others show them how cells work and how DNA affects processes such as digestion and reproduction. **WHAT** they do here must be carried out under strict conditions.

CONFUSED CRICKETS

Crickets chirp around sunrise and sunset. But streetlights left on all night in cities might be affecting their natural rhythm. To find out the impact that artificial lights have on insects, this zoologist has set up an experiment: what will happen to the crickets living in tanks where the light is left on all day, compared to those left mostly in the dark?

AMPHIBIAN ANSWERS

This zoologist is testing small amounts of water taken from hundreds of ponds up and down the country. A computer will scan the water in each test tube for tiny fragments of amphibian DNA. The zoologist hopes to find out which ponds are home to frogs, toads and salamanders.

ANTI-ANTS

To communicate, many animals use smells called pheromones. This zoologist is applying a pheromone near this rotting fruit. If it scares ants away, they may have discovered a natural ant repellent that could be used in houses where ants have become troublesome pests.

BEHOLD: THE VINEGAR FLY!

No animal has done more to further zoology than the humble vinegar fly, *Drosophila melanogaster*. It is easy to keep in a laboratory, so scientists know lots about its DNA. This incredible insect has helped us learn more about how animal characteristics and behaviours are passed down through generations. This area of science is called genetics.

TRANSFORMING TECHNOLOGIES

Today, the computers found in many laboratories can search through DNA with lightning speed. This efficiency helps laboratories share their findings with others very quickly, increasing the rate at which discoveries are made. Here are a few reasons **WHY** these findings are so crucial to future science.

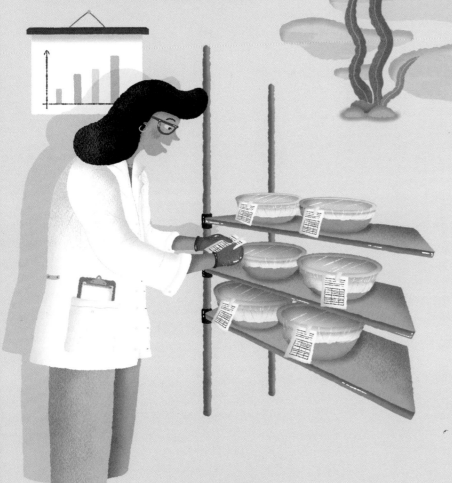

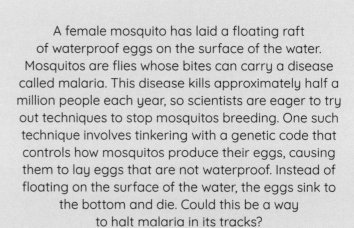

A female mosquito has laid a floating raft of waterproof eggs on the surface of the water. Mosquitos are flies whose bites can carry a disease called malaria. This disease kills approximately half a million people each year, so scientists are eager to try out techniques to stop mosquitos breeding. One such technique involves tinkering with a genetic code that controls how mosquitos produce their eggs, causing them to lay eggs that are not waterproof. Instead of floating on the surface of the water, the eggs sink to the bottom and die. Could this be a way to halt malaria in its tracks?

STILL TO SOLVE: WHY DO WE SLEEP?

All animals go through periods of reduced brain activity, which we call sleep. But why? See-through nematode worms may hold the answer. Scientists identified a molecule that causes the worms to sleep, then altered the genes of certain worms so that they cannot produce it. The sleepless worms struggled to recover from periods of intense stress, such as cold weather or drought. Somehow, sleep recharges our bodies. But how does sleep do this? That's for future zoologists to try to answer!

Each year, some 20 million tonnes of plastic waste seeps into the world's oceans. Zoologists are looking for animals that can help by consuming the plastic waste that humans produce. One candidate is the humble mealworm, the grub of a small beetle farmed for pet food. Not only can mealworms consume many types of plastic, they can also digest toxic chemicals found in plastics and change them, during digestion, into non-toxic ingredients. This means that mealworms fed on plastic can be fed to other animals, including livestock, without poisoning them.

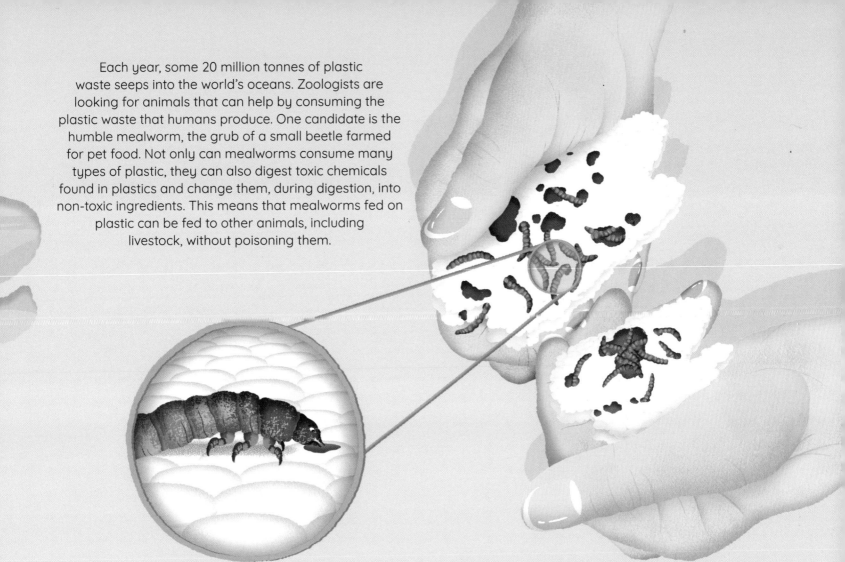

NEW TO SCIENCE

Decades ago, zoologists exploring Indonesia's tropical islands came face-to-face with a small mammal called a tarsier. Suspecting it to be a new species, scientists recorded its calls and took samples of its DNA, to compare with other tarsiers. It took 25 years, but it was finally deemed different enough to be its own species. In 2019, it was named Niemitz's tarsier after one of the zoologists who first observed it, all those years ago.

UNDERSEA HORROR

Millions of years ago, invertebrates ruled the oceans. In this display case is *Jaekelopterus* (pronounced yake-elop-ter-us), a crocodile-sized predator that hunted fish in lakes and rivers. It may have been the largest armoured invertebrate ever – its claws were longer than chair legs!

BIRD BUDDIES

Many birds have, living in their feathers, spider-like hitchhikers known as feather mites. There are more than 2,500 species of feather mite and some birds host their own unique species.

CLUES TO THE PAST

Palaeontology is the study of prehistoric animals, plants and even fungi. But many palaeontologists study modern-day animals too, to understand the basics of how animals work and apply those principles to long-lost species.

Museums

Cabinet after cabinet of curious critters! Across the world, museums store more than 100 million animal objects like bones, fossils and dead specimens, specially treated so that they do not decay. Many of these items are on display to all **WHO** wish to explore the natural world as it was millions of years ago.

SUPER SHARK

Megalodon, a giant prehistoric shark, shut its jaws with ten times the power of a great white shark. This, along with its razor-sharp teeth, helped the super-predator crush the bones of whales, its favourite prey.

BEAVER BURROWS

For almost a century, no one knew what made the strange corkscrew fossils like the one in this display case. Scientists now know that they were the burrows of an extinct species of beaver, *Palaeocastor*. Fossils of an animal's impact on its environment, rather than the animal itself, are called trace fossils.

MUSEUM MODEL

This fossilised footprint is the size of a jacuzzi! It was made 130 million years ago by a sauropod, a long-necked dinosaur, walking through mudflats in what is today Walmadan, a region of Australia. The fossils are too large to remove from the rock where they were found, so this is a carefully prepared model.

HOW DO ANIMAL FOSSILS FORM?

Most fossils are of hard body parts like bones. This is because, when an animal dies, these are the bits that scavenging animals find hardest to eat. If an animal dies and is buried in grainy sediment, such as mud or ash, the hard body parts can remain for hundreds of thousands of years. During this period, they become replaced by minerals, which gives fossils their shiny, crystal-like appearance. Most fossils are still underground, waiting to be found by future scientists.

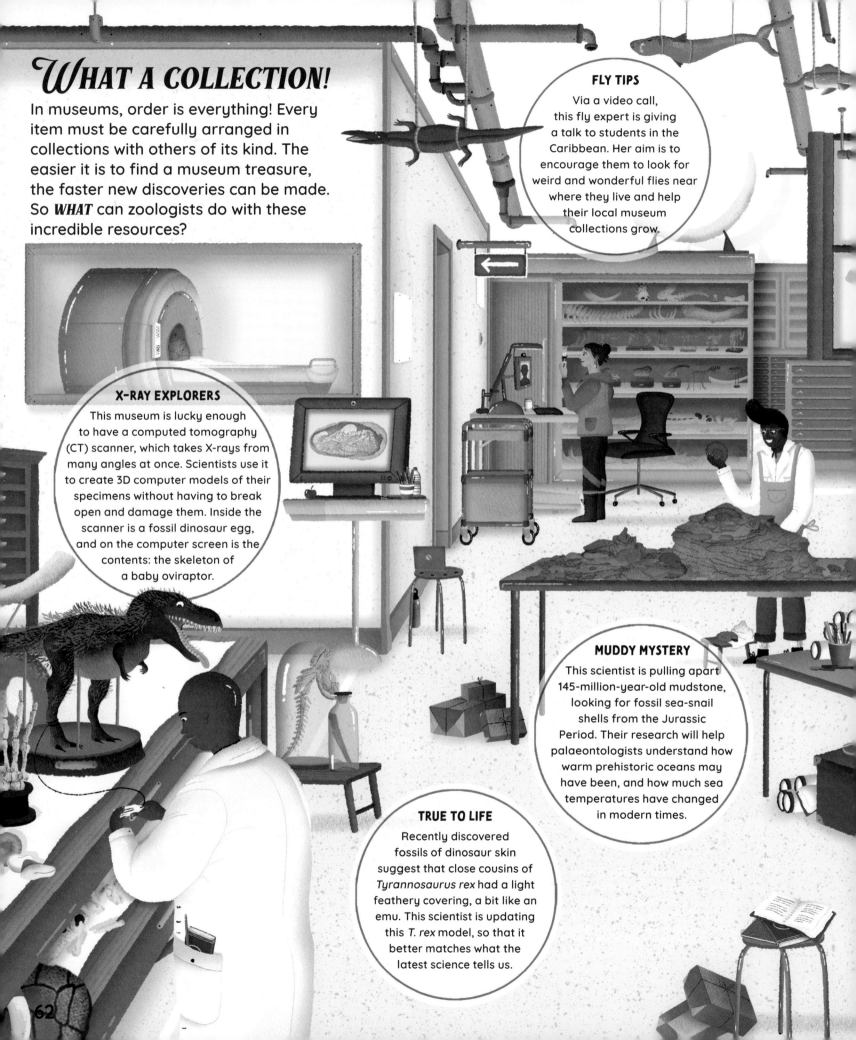

WHAT A COLLECTION!

In museums, order is everything! Every item must be carefully arranged in collections with others of its kind. The easier it is to find a museum treasure, the faster new discoveries can be made. So **WHAT** can zoologists do with these incredible resources?

FLY TIPS

Via a video call, this fly expert is giving a talk to students in the Caribbean. Her aim is to encourage them to look for weird and wonderful flies near where they live and help their local museum collections grow.

X-RAY EXPLORERS

This museum is lucky enough to have a computed tomography (CT) scanner, which takes X-rays from many angles at once. Scientists use it to create 3D computer models of their specimens without having to break open and damage them. Inside the scanner is a fossil dinosaur egg, and on the computer screen is the contents: the skeleton of a baby oviraptor.

MUDDY MYSTERY

This scientist is pulling apart 145-million-year-old mudstone, looking for fossil sea-snail shells from the Jurassic Period. Their research will help palaeontologists understand how warm prehistoric oceans may have been, and how much sea temperatures have changed in modern times.

TRUE TO LIFE

Recently discovered fossils of dinosaur skin suggest that close cousins of *Tyrannosaurus rex* had a light feathery covering, a bit like an emu. This scientist is updating this *T. rex* model, so that it better matches what the latest science tells us.

SKULL SEARCH

This zoologist is measuring the length of fox skulls collected more than 100 years ago. He will compare the measurements with modern-day foxes to see whether the shape of the fox skull has evolved in the last 100 years to help them to eat a new diet: human rubbish.

WHAT IS TAXONOMY?

Taxonomy is the branch of science that sorts living organisms into families, genuses, species and other groups. To assign an animal to the right group, taxonomists look at skeletons, body parts, colour patterns and, increasingly, DNA codes. If an animal has features that are very different to others, the scientists may have a new species on their hands.

CAREFUL COLLECTORS

This zoologist is carefully rearranging the museum's beetle collection. Drawer after drawer of thousands of different beetles have been put in order and each individual specimen has been given a unique barcode, so it can be easily found later.

LESSONS FROM THE PAST

In many parts of the world, climate change is affecting the timing of spring. Here, a zoologist is looking through 200-year-old zoology books from the museum library to find out when frogs laid their eggs back then, and compare this to when they lay their eggs today.

CATHEDRALS TO NATURE

How did life begin on Earth? Why did the largest dinosaurs go extinct but not crocodiles and mammals? And how did humans evolve? Museum collections hold the answers to questions like these – that's **WHY** they're so vital to a zoologist's work.

Many rocks are made from grainy bits called sediments. Often, sediments are made from old mud and sands which are laid down, layer-upon-layer, over many millions of years. These layers are called strata. Each stratum has different fossils inside, depending on the animals that lived at the time. This means that, working together, geologists (rock scientists) and palaeontologists can dig through the strata to travel back in time, using fossils to find out what lived at different times in Earth's history.

Fossils tell us that, at five points in Earth's long history, there have been periods when many types of animals went extinct all at once. These mass extinction events include the giant meteorite that killed off the largest dinosaurs, and events long before. The worst mass extinction event was the 'Great Dying' that occurred 250 million years ago, when nine out of ten ocean species and over two-thirds of life on land faced extinction. Like detectives, palaeontologists search for clues about what may have caused mass extinction events like this. Their findings might help us in the fight against climate change.

These lumps of earwax were collected long ago from whales that were washed ashore and died. Today, they are being scanned for polluting chemicals, such as mercury, found in the water when the whales were alive. Museum specimens like these can tell us about pollution levels 100 years or more in the past, helping us to understand the impact that humans have on the oceans. When it was first collected, no one could have predicted how useful to science this earwax would be!

NEW TO SCIENCE

When dinosaurs ruled the land, *Kyhytysuka* (pronounced ki-hit-ee-su-ka) ruled the seas! With a skull 1 metre in length and jaws laced with fierce cone-shaped teeth, this marine reptile hunted large fish and possibly small dinosaurs that strayed too close to the water. Fossils from this newly described species were first discovered by scientists in Colombia. The name means 'the one that cuts with something sharp' in a local indigenous language.

BACK FROM THE BRINK

By building up their numbers in zoos and carefully releasing them back into the wild, some large animals have been successfully saved from extinction. Fifty years ago, the population of Mongolian wild horses was down to a handful of individuals, but captive breeding in zoos has helped their numbers to recover. Today, 1,200 Mongolian wild horses live wild across Mongolia, China and Russia.

SEA OTTER SURPRISES

Sea otters have a special pouch in each armpit where they store seafood snacks for later. Some sea otters also keep a special rock in one of their pouches, which they use to crack open shellfish. Like us, most sea otters are right-handed.

CLEVER KOMODOS

In the wild, the 3-metre long Komodo dragon likes to swim between tropical islands, searching for food. Should an island have plenty of deer to eat, the female Komodo dragon has a special trick. Without need for a male, she can produce a clutch of eggs that contain baby versions of her. This means she can start a family on an island all by herself. This behaviour, called parthenogenesis, was first observed in a zoo.

PANDA PONG

To wee as high as possible up this tree stump, this panda is doing a handstand. The higher up the tree its urine splashes, the more other pandas will smell it. During the mating season, pandas spend lots of time marking their territories in this way. This lets other pandas know that, nearby, there is a panda in the mood for love.

ZOOS AND AQUARIUMS

The best zoos work together to use their collections for a common cause – to save animals from extinction! To do this, they work closely with zoologists around the world, who tell them how wild animals are doing and what zoos can do to help. Many of the animals **WHO** are cared for in zoos are among the most endangered on Earth.

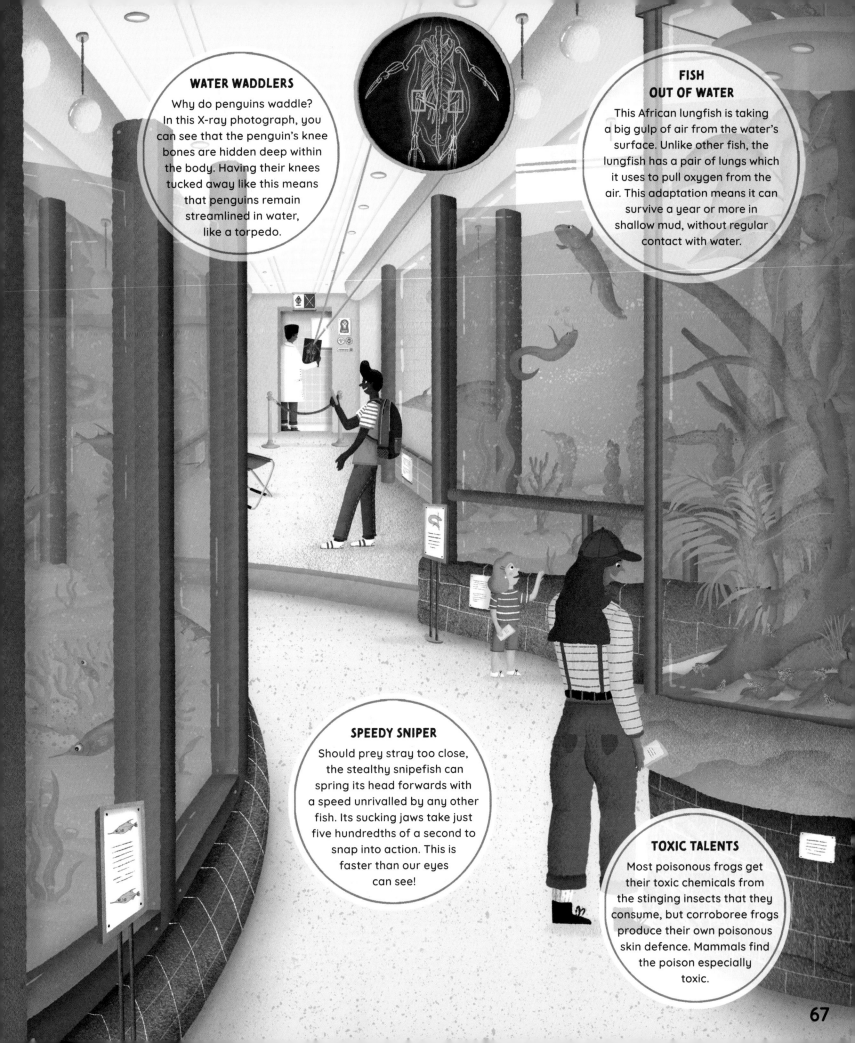

WATER WADDLERS

Why do penguins waddle? In this X-ray photograph, you can see that the penguin's knee bones are hidden deep within the body. Having their knees tucked away like this means that penguins remain streamlined in water, like a torpedo.

FISH OUT OF WATER

This African lungfish is taking a big gulp of air from the water's surface. Unlike other fish, the lungfish has a pair of lungs which it uses to pull oxygen from the air. This adaptation means it can survive a year or more in shallow mud, without regular contact with water.

SPEEDY SNIPER

Should prey stray too close, the stealthy snipefish can spring its head forwards with a speed unrivalled by any other fish. Its sucking jaws take just five hundredths of a second to snap into action. This is faster than our eyes can see!

TOXIC TALENTS

Most poisonous frogs get their toxic chemicals from the stinging insects that they consume, but corroboree frogs produce their own poisonous skin defence. Mammals find the poison especially toxic.

CLEAN-UP

These seabirds are covered in oil. They were brought to the zoo after an oil spill at sea affected their habitat. As well as making flight impossible, oil stops their feathers locking together to form a warm, insulated coat. To treat the birds, zoologists and vets are bathing them using special shampoos.

PUPPET SHOW

These zoologists are using a condor puppet to feed this chick strips of meat. The puppet limits the condor chick's contact with humans, helping the chick understand that it is a bird, not a person. Techniques like this give the chick the best chance of survival, once it is old enough to be released into the wild.

PARROT PUZZLES

Parrots are very intelligent. Some African grey parrots can understand concepts such as colours, numbers and even sentences. To keep parrots like these from becoming bored, zoologists think up lots of clever games for them to play. This parrot is playing with a puzzle box in which food has been hidden – can it use the stick to pull out the food?

GUARDIANS OF THE GOING, GOING, GOING

To keep the animals in their care as happy and healthy as possible, zoologists spend lots of time monitoring animal diets and researching their behaviours. **WHAT** zoologists do in zoos helps them learn about the needs of animals, so that they can do an even better job of looking after them in future.

RAT ROYALTY

Most rats live just two or three years, but the naked mole rat can live 30 years or more. That means that the queen of this colony has been around longer than many of the zookeepers! Scientists think mole rats live this long because of special chemicals in their blood, which lessen the impact of toxic atoms in their cells. This zoologist is collecting samples of DNA from naked mole rat poo to find out more.

BETTER BREEDING

Zoos work hard to make sure the healthiest individuals in their care get to breed with other healthy individuals. Often, this means that animals are swapped between zoos for months or years at a time. Careful planning like this means that, when they are reintroduced into the wild, the animals are ready to go.

NEXT GENERATION

This zoologist is giving a talk to a group of schoolchildren about her favourite animal: frogs! She hopes that talks like these will inspire children to become more involved in wildlife conservation.

MIRROR, MIRROR

This pygmy slow loris has just had a mirror installed in its enclosure and the zoologists are interested to see how it responds. Will it be surprised and think that the reflection is an intruder, or will it recognise itself in the reflection? Zoologists use mirrors to test whether animals understand their own existence in the same way that humans do.

ℛETURNING THE RARE

WHY are zoos so important to scientific research? By working closely with the animals in their care, zoologists gain knowledge and experience that can be applied to animals in the wild, helping to protect them for future generations. Many zoo animals are carefully reared in order to one day be released back into the wild.

When zoo-reared golden lion tamarins are released back into the Amazon rainforest, it takes a long time for them to feel confident in the wild. First, under watchful eyes, zoologists let the small monkeys get used to a safe enclosure in the rainforest, where there is food. As their confidence grows, the tamarins explore the rainforest, running back to the enclosure whenever they are scared. Within months, the tamarins feel at home in their new surroundings. Zoologists continue to monitor their progress for more than a year, following their movements using radio trackers attached to tiny collars. In the last 40 years, 146 golden lion tamarins have been reintroduced into the wild – a complicated operation that involved 43 zoos!

These freezers contain DNA from thousands of zoo species, each with their own unique barcode. This DNA helps zoos to keep track of the animals in their care and, one day, could even be used to bring extinct zoo specimens back to life. To make sure the DNA isn't damaged by heat and light, samples are stored in special freezers at -80°C – that's colder than an average winter's night in Antarctica!

Some zoos help species whose populations are plummeting very quickly by providing them a temporary place to live. One example is the rare fen raft spider, whose wetland habitats were in danger of drying out. To help the species, some zoos took in thousands of baby spiders, kept in test tubes and fed on a daily diet of flies. Once they became adults, the spiders were released in new nature reserves, where they were able to flourish.

Zoologists caring for baby pandas often dress up in panda costumes and wear a special perfume... made from panda wee! This stops pandas associating humans with food, a problem that can cause the gentle giants to seek out villages and towns after being released into the wild. By hiding their scent, carers hope that the pandas will stick to their natural foraging behaviour.

NEW TO SCIENCE

While looking after the fish at the aquarium of Schönbrunn Zoo, Austria, a zoologist noticed a tiny shrimp living at the bottom of a tank. Convinced it was a new species, the zoologist set about comparing its bristly body with 107 closely related shrimp species. The shrimp turned out to be so unique that it was, in 2021, given its own species name, *Heteromysis schoenbrunnensis*.

ZOOLOGY FOR ALL!

Zoology isn't just for grown-ups, it's for everyone! No matter your age, there are lots of ways you can begin your zoological adventures within metres of where you live. It's time to explore...

HIDE AND SEEK

Woodlice and small beetles like to hide underneath small rocks and branches, where it's nice and damp. Count them and see how their numbers go up and down according to the seasons. Sometimes, you might discover lurking predators such as hungry centipedes or spiders with large, crushing jaws. Where do they hide? How do they hunt? Use a torch to watch what they get up to at night.

LOOKING FOR FOOTPRINTS

Animal footprints are like secret signposts. Best observed in mud, sand or snow, they can be identified easily to help you learn more about animals that live in your neighbourhood. How many toes do they have? Are the tracks heavy or light? In what direction do they go? Questions like these will hone your zoological detective skills.

MAKE A MUSEUM

Feathers, shells, fossils, fur; collecting items like these and storing them carefully in a drawer or a display at home can help you keep a record of the animals that live (or lived long ago) near you. Mini-museums like these can be very inspiring – some zoologists still cherish their childhood collections.

TUNE IN YOUR EARS

Birdsong is like a secret radio station that only animal-lovers can tune into. Start by learning basic bird calls. Then, listen for short, sharp whistles that these birds make to alert one another of danger. When you hear alarm calls like these, scan the air for predators nearby. You might catch a glimpse of a spectacular hawk or falcon, or a fox hiding in nearby bushes, ready to pounce.

SPEND TIME WITH A FLOWER

A flower is like a service station for passing insects. Hundreds of different species depend on them for sugary nectar. In sunny weather, take a moment to sit next to a flower and watch what comes and goes. Within minutes you'll see pollinating hoverflies, flower beetles, bees and day-flying moths. Wait longer and you might see their predators: dragonflies, wasps and even camouflaged crab spiders!

CITIZEN SCIENCE

Sometimes, to find out more about how habitats are changing, scientists ask thousands of people to count the birds in their street or the insects on their flowers during a given time. Getting lots of data like this, over months or years, means that scientists can see changes in animal numbers more clearly. As well as helping scientists understand wildlife populations, this 'citizen science' can offer young zoologists early experience of some amazing wildlife conservation projects.

Here's to the Future!

There are thousands of animal mysteries yet to be solved. Hundreds of thousands of fossils, waiting to be dug up. Millions of unknown species, not yet described. Are you up to the job of finding out more? Then the life of a zoologist awaits!

Here, some of the greatest zoologists alive offer you their advice on getting into zoology. Good luck!

Catalina Pimiento,
SHARK SCIENTIST

'The less you know about something and the quicker you admit it, the more you can learn. Learning something new is the basis of science and it feels great.'

Keneiloe Molopyane,
ZOOLOGIST STUDYING HUMAN ORIGINS

'Don't only ask questions. Go out and find the answers to those questions. This is the essence of science and exploration, and honestly where the most fun and fulfilment can be found.'

Kenji Suetsugu,
INSECT ZOOLOGIST

'I believe that there are always interesting discoveries to be made if you take the time to observe even the most everyday animals. I urge you to take the time to observe the animals around you!'

Huw Griffiths,
ZOOLOGIST IN ANTARCTICA

'Don't let anyone tell you that you can't turn your passion for nature into an amazing career. Also, don't leave a jar with 100 snails in it, without a lid on, in your parents' house, it will only get you in trouble!'

Priscilla Wehi,
CONSERVATION BIOLOGIST

'Look closely. You will see amazing things that you may want to write about – poetry, stories, music. Telling stories is an awesome part of what we do as scientists!'

GABI FLEURY.
CARNIVORE BIOLOGIST

'Start learning about wildlife at home! There are so many animals to be found, even in cities and in your own backyard! Read widely, study hard at school and stay curious about the natural world.'

HANA AYOOB.
MAKER OF ZOOLOGY STAGE-SHOWS

'Even if you can't handle animals or be outside much, there are still lots of opportunities to work in zoology-related fields and to share your love for animals.'

JACK ASHBY.
MUSEUM ZOOLOGIST

'Out in the world, be it a patch of brambles or a whole forest, just stop and watch – take notice of what everything is doing and try and work out why.'

ADAM HART.
INSECT ZOOLOGIST

'There's as much to learn from a caterpillar as an elephant or an ant nest under a stone as a tiger. It's all nature and it's all amazing.'

NSA DADA.
MOSQUITO ZOOLOGIST

'Explore your curiosity; ask questions, read and explore resources about what you love. Don't be afraid or ashamed to get outside and get your hands dirty, there's so much to explore and learn out there.'

DANI RABAIOTTI.
WILD DOG ZOOLOGIST

'Get some practical skills! Either outdoor skills if you want to work outdoors, computing skills if research takes your fancy, or writing skills if you prefer that route!'

Glossary

APOSEMATISM

A defence mechanism used by animals where their colouring is reflective of how dangerous they are

CLIMATE CHANGE

The gradual change in weather patterns

COLONY

A large group of insects living together in a nest

COMPUTER TOMOGRAPHY (CT) SCANNER

A scanner that uses X-rays to create a detailed image

CONVERGENT EVOLUTION

When different animals evolve in the same way, despite not being related

DEFORESTATION

Deliberate clearing of forests for fuel or farmland

DNA

Genetic information that is unique to each organism

ECHOLOCATION

The use of soundwaves by animals to detect surrounding objects

ECO-FRIENDLY

Activity that does not harm the environment

ECOSYSTEM

The plants and animals of a particular environment

ECOTOURISM

Tourism that does not harm, change or impact the local environment in any way

EVOLUTION

The adaptation of species to their environment over time

EXTINCTION

The dying out of a species or group

FOOD CHAIN

A network of animals and plants that are dependent on each other to survive

FOSSIL

The preserved remains or impressions of something once living that have hardened into rock

GENETICS

The characteristics of organisms passed from parents to their offspring

GENUS

Species that are closely related, like dogs and wolves

GRASSLANDS

An area where the dominant plant is grass

GRUB

The larva of an insect

HABITAT

The natural home of a plant or animal

HERBIVORE

An animal that does not eat meat and lives off plants to survive

HYDROTHERMAL VENT

An opening in the sea floor out of which hot water flows

INVERTEBRATE

An animal without a backbone

MAMMAL

A warm-blooded animal that has hair, whose females can feed babies with their own milk

MICROSCOPIC

So small as to be visible only under a microscope

MIGRATION

The seasonal movement of animals from one location to another

ORGANISM

A living thing that consists of more than one cell

PARTHENOGENESIS

A reproductive process in which a female animal produces babies without needing a male

PHOTOPHORE

A type of animal cell that produces light

POLYP

A tiny invertebrate that lives in the sea, and forms coral reefs with colonies of other polyps

PREDATOR

An animal that lives by killing and eating other animals

REPTILE

A cold-blooded animal that breathes air and lays eggs (mostly)

SPECIMEN

An animal, plant or object used as an example and for study

SEDIMENT

The remains of plants, animals and rocks that have been moved by wind, water or air and settled in a new location, like sand

SPECIES

A group of organisms that can breed with one another

STRATUM

A layer of sediment

SYMBIOSIS

A beneficial relationship between two different species that helps each to survive

TALON

A sharp claw of a bird of prey

TEMPERATE

Having mild temperatures

TRIANGULATION

A method of finding an exact location by forming triangles to it from other locations

VENOM

A poison administered by an animal, often by stinging or biting

VERTEBRATE

An animal that has a backbone

ZOOLOGIST

A scientist who studies animals

ZOOLOGY

The scientific study of animals